HENRY AND MUDGE

BEST FRIENDS
FOREVER

HENRY AND MUDGE

BEST FRIENDS FOREVER

by Cynthia Rylant

Henry and Mudge and Annie's Perfect Pet
and *Henry and Mudge and the Snowman Plan*
illustrated by Suçie Stevenson

Henry and Mudge and the Tall Tree House,
Henry and Mudge and the Wild Goose Chase,
and *Henry and Mudge and the Funny Lunch*
illustrated by Carolyn Bracken
in the style of Suçie Stevenson

READY–TO–READ

ALADDIN PAPERBACKS
New York   London   Toronto   Sydney

THE HENRY AND MUDGE BOOKS

ALADDIN PAPERBACKS
An imprint of Simon & Schuster Children's Publishing Division
1230 Avenue of the Americas, New York, NY 10020
Henry and Mudge and the Tall Tree House
Text copyright © 2002 by Cynthia Rylant. Illustrations copyright © 2002 by Suçie Stevenson.
Henry and Mudge and Annie's Perfect Pet
Text copyright © 2000 by Cynthia Rylant. Illustrations copyright © 2000 by Suçie Stevenson.
Henry and Mudge and the Snowman Plan
Text copyright © 1999 by Cynthia Rylant. Illustrations copyright © 1999 by Suçie Stevenson.
Henry and Mudge and the Wild Goose Chase
Text copyright © 2003 by Cynthia Rylant. Illustrations copyright © 2003 by Suçie Stevenson.
Henry and Mudge and the Funny Lunch
Text copyright © 2004 by Cynthia Rylant. Illustrations copyright © 2004 by Suçie Stevenson.
Henry and Mudge and the Tall Tree House, *Henry and Mudge and Annie's Perfect Pet*, *Henry and Mudge and the Snowman Plan*, *Henry and Mudge and the Wild Goose Chase*, and *Henry and Mudge and the Funny Lunch* were previously published individually by Aladdin Paperbacks.

ALADDIN PAPERBACKS, READY-TO-READ, and colophon are registered trademarks of Simon & Schuster, Inc.
The text of this book was set in 18 point Goudy.
The illustrations were rendered in pen-and-ink and watercolor.
This March 2006 Aladdin Paperbacks edition created exclusively for Barnes & Noble Publishing, Inc. under
ISBN-13: 978-0-7607-7538-7
ISBN-10: 0-7607-7538-9.
Printed and bound in the United States of America
07 08 LBM 9 8 7 6 5 4 3

Contents

Henry and Mudge
and the
Tall Tree House

To Joe and Dean, good uncles—CR

Contents

4

Uncle Jake

One day Uncle Jake
came to visit Henry
and Henry's big dog, Mudge,
and Henry's parents.

Uncle Jake was very big.
Henry's father called him "burly."
"What does 'burly' mean?"
Henry asked his father.
"Big, hairy, and plaid,"
said Henry's father.

That was Uncle Jake.

Henry liked Uncle Jake a lot.
Mudge liked him even more.
Mudge liked Uncle Jake
because Uncle Jake *wrestled*.

Mudge and Uncle Jake
would get on the floor
and wrestle and wrestle.

Mudge always won.

This time when Uncle Jake
came to visit,
he had something special
in his truck.
He had boards.
"What are the boards for,
Uncle Jake?" asked Henry.

Uncle Jake gave a burly smile and said,
"Adventure."

"Really?" said Henry.

He liked adventure.

Especially with Mudge.

"Yep, I'm building you a *tree house*,"

said Uncle Jake.

"A tree house?" said Henry. "Wow!"
Henry loved tree houses.
They were thrilling.
They were exciting.
They were . . . *in trees*.

Henry looked at Mudge.

Mudge could jump.

Mudge could run.

Mudge could even
dance a little.

14

But Mudge, for sure, could not
climb a tree.
"Uh-oh," thought Henry.
He put his arm around Mudge
and began to worry.

The Tree House

Uncle Jake was so burly
that he had the tree house
built in two hours.
He and Henry and Mudge
stood beneath it.

17

Uncle Jake was very proud.
Henry was very worried.
Mudge was just itchy.
"Okay, Henry, it's all yours,"
said Uncle Jake.
"Go on up!"

Henry looked at Mudge.
Henry did not want
to go into the tree house.
He did not want adventure
without Mudge.
But he couldn't hurt
Uncle Jake's feelings.
He climbed up.

19

He stood in the
tree house
and looked around.
It was thrilling.
It was exciting.
It was *lonely*.
"Thanks, Uncle Jake,"
Henry called.
"It's great."

21

"I'll take Mudge
for a walk,"
said Uncle Jake.
"Have a ball!"
Henry watched Mudge
leave with Uncle Jake.

22

Mudge didn't want to go.
Henry could tell because
Mudge kept sitting down
and yawning.
Mudge always acted tired
when he didn't want to go.
"Sleepy dog!" Uncle Jake
called with a smile.

24

Finally he got Mudge
down the road.
And Henry felt sadder
than any boy with a
new tree house ever felt.

Forgot Something

Henry sat in his tree house
for fourteen minutes.
Then he climbed down
and went into the house.
Uncle Jake was back.
He and Henry's parents
were playing cards.

"I forgot something!"
Henry told them.
He ran upstairs.
Mudge was on Henry's bed,
chewing a bone.
Henry gave Mudge
a big hug and kiss
and ran back downstairs.

He waved to his parents
and Uncle Jake, then
returned to the tree house.

He sat
for fourteen minutes.

31

Then he climbed down and went
into the house.
"Forgot something else!"
he called.

He ran upstairs.

He came back down.

He returned to the tree house
for fourteen more minutes.

Then he climbed back down and went
into the house.
"Forgot something!"
He did the same thing over and over.
Five times in a row.

Finally Henry's father
met him at the door.
"Henry, what *is* it?"
asked Henry's father.
Henry hung his head.
"I miss Mudge."
Henry's father smiled.
"I thought you might,"
he said.
"So Uncle Jake and I
came up with a plan."

Very Happy

"Isn't this great, Mudge?"
asked Henry.
They were sitting in
the tree house.
They had comic books
and cheese sandwiches.
Mudge had some toys:
a bear, an alligator,
and a roly-poly snowman.
They were very happy.
A tree house in a tree was okay.

But a tree house in Henry's room
was even better!
It was thrilling.
It was exciting.

It had Mudge.

Henry and Mudge
AND
Annie's Perfect Pet

Contents

Annie's Wish

Henry and Henry's big dog Mudge
always visited Cousin Annie
next door.
Annie used to live far away.
Henry didn't see much of her.
But now she lived next door
and it was fun!

Henry and Annie rode bikes,
played Frisbee, and
traded comics.

And, of course, they petted Mudge
all the time.

Annie loved Mudge.
She loved his soft eyes
and his warm nose
and his big paws.
Annie wished she had a dog.

But her father was at work
every day.
No one would be home
to take care of a dog.
Henry felt sorry for Annie.
He remembered how much fun it was
to get a new pet.

Mudge had been the cutest puppy.

He was all round and rolly.

And very small.

Henry could pick him up

and kiss him.

Henry sure couldn't
do that now!

And Mudge was so short
that he could walk *under*
the collie down the street.

Not anymore!
Henry wanted Annie to
have her own pet.
He went to his parents
for help.

Soft and Dry

"Maybe she could
get a mouse," said Henry's father.
"Annie's afraid of mice,"
said Henry.

"What about a turtle?"
said Henry's mother.
"Too wet for Annie,"
said Henry.

"A crab?" said his father.

"Too hard," said Henry.

"A bird?" said his mother.

Henry shook his head.

"It might fly into

Annie's teacups," he said.

"Okay," said Henry's father,
"Annie needs a pet that
isn't scary, isn't wet,
isn't hard, doesn't fly,
and tap-dances."
"*Tap-dances?*" Henry giggled.
"I just threw that one in,"
said Henry's dad.

Henry's mother was thinking.
"I know!" she said. "A bunny!
It's soft and dry and
doesn't fly."
"And it doesn't have to be
walked like a dog," said Henry.

"Yes," said Henry's father,
"but can it dance?"

The Pet Store

Henry and Henry's parents
and Henry's big dog Mudge
took Annie to the pet store.
When they went inside,
birds were singing,
puppies were barking,
kittens were meowing,
and mice were squeaking.

But the bunnies
in the corner
were being quiet.
Quiet and careful.
Just like Annie.
"Perfect," said Henry's mother.

Annie picked up a
white baby bunny.
She had soft eyes,
just like Mudge.
She had a warm nose,
just like Mudge.

And she had something

Mudge didn't:

a little cottontail.

"She's so *cute!*" Annie said with a smile.

Mudge put his warm nose
up to the bunny's warm nose.
The bunny sniffed, sniffed, sniffed.
She seemed to like Mudge.

And when Mudge gave her
a big drooly kiss,
she didn't even mind.

Henry looked at his parents.
"We've found Annie's perfect pet,"
he said.
And they took the
bunny home.

Snowball

Henry's Uncle Ed made
a beautiful hutch for
Annie's bunny.

It was painted with
flowers and trees.
It had a little china bowl
for the bunny to eat from.
And soft bits of cotton
for the bunny to sleep on.
It fit Annie's room perfectly.

Annie named her bunny Snowball.
She played with her,
and sang to her,
and took her to Henry's house
for visits.

The bunny liked Henry's house.

She liked riding on Mudge's back.

Mudge carried the bunny

all around.

And when he got tired, they
stopped for crackers.

Annie was so happy
to have a pet.
A pet just right for her.
"I love my bunny," Annie
told Henry.
"I know," Henry said. "She's soft
and dry and doesn't fly."

Suddenly the bunny went flying
through the air and landed
on Mudge's back.
Annie laughed.
"Maybe she *does*!" she said.

Henry and Mudge
AND THE
Snowman Plan

For Samantha J. Wills—CR

For Benjamin Brown especially, and also for Joshua and Dennis Brown, and for Amy van der Clock Brown—SS

Contents

Contest!

On a snowy day in January,
Henry and Henry's big dog Mudge
saw a sign in a store window.
It said SNOWMAN CONTEST,
SATURDAY AT THE PARK.

"A snowman contest!"
said Henry. "Wow!"
Mudge wagged his tail.
He always wagged his tail
when Henry said, "Wow."
It meant excitement.

And sometimes it meant
dessert!
Henry ran home
to tell his father.

Henry's father was in the
basement, painting a chair.
He had green paint on his
hair, across his nose,
and in his mustache.

"Guess what, Dad?" said Henry.

(Mudge was looking for a

special old boot.)

"What?" asked Henry's father.

He wiped some paint across his chin.

"There's a snowman contest on
Saturday!" said Henry.

"Snowman contest!" said Henry's
father. He wiped some paint
on his ears. "Wow!"

"Can we go?" asked Henry.

"Sure!" said Henry's father.

He wiped some paint on his elbow.

Henry looked at his father.

Henry looked at the chair.

"Dad, I think that chair has been painting *you*," said Henry.

Henry's dad looked at himself
in an old mirror.
He had green hair, a green nose,
a green mustache, a green chin,
green ears, and a green elbow.
Henry's dad looked at Henry.
He said, "You should see me
when I paint a *house*!"

At the Park

On Saturday, Henry and
Henry's father and
Henry's big dog Mudge
went to the park.
There were many people there.

All of the people had things.

They had shovels and spoons.

They had hats and shoes.

They had rocks and carrots
and marbles and broccoli.
"Broccoli?" said Henry
to his father.

And, of course, they all had dogs.

"It looks more like a

wagging contest to me,"

said Henry's father.

Mudge wagged and wagged.

Henry and his dad had already
made their snowman plan.
They looked at each other.
They shook hands.
"Good luck, break a leg,
and don't let the bedbugs bite,"
said Henry's father.
And they got to work.

KITTY
LITTER

While Henry and his father built
their snowman, Mudge visited.
He visited a poodle.

He visited a husky.

He visited a dachshund

who didn't want to visit him.

Then he found a carrot to
chew on.
A Chihuahua helped him chew it.
Mudge finished his half first.

It looked like the Chihuahua
might finish hers
sometime in July.
Mudge wagged and
gave her a kiss.

Snow Aliens

By 3:00 all of the snowmen
were ready for the judges.
Henry and his father
looked around the park.

There were snowpeople.

There were snowcats.

There were snowdogs.

There were snow aliens.

And one person had built
a snow Abraham Lincoln.
"Wow!" said Henry.

The judges walked all around.

Henry was feeling nervous.

He held Mudge's collar.

Holding Mudge's collar

always helped when

Henry was nervous.

"I hope they like ours,"
Henry said.
"Me too," said Henry's dad,
holding Mudge's collar
on the other side.

Finally the judges arrived.

They looked carefully at the snowman Henry and his father had built.

They looked at the front.

They looked at the back.

They looked all around.

Finally one of them asked,

"What is it?"

"It's my dad when he's painting

a chair," said Henry.

The judges looked again
and laughed and laughed.
Mudge wagged and drooled
on their boots.

When the winners were
announced, first place went
to Abraham Lincoln.
Second place went to a
snow leopard.

And third place went to
the snowman with paint
in his mustache.
"Yay!" yelled Henry.
Henry and Henry's father
proudly looked at their prizes.

One was a purple ribbon.

It said THIRD PLACE WINNER,

MOST ORIGINAL SNOWMAN.

And the other prize was

a big box of snowman cookies.

"I sure am glad you're a
messy painter, Dad,"
said Henry.
"I'm an even messier *eater*,"
said Henry's father.

And he and Henry
and Henry's big dog Mudge
took their prizes home and
made a wonderful cookie mess.

HENRY AND MUDGE
AND THE
WILD GOOSE CHASE

Contents

Farm Fresh

One day Henry's mother told
Henry and Henry's father
that she wanted some
"farm-fresh eggs."

Henry imagined a plate full
of farm-fresh eggs.
"Yum," he said.
Mudge wagged.
He always wagged at "yum."

Then Henry's mother said
she wanted some
fresh-picked blueberries.
"Yum **yum**," said Henry.
Mudge wagged harder.
"Yum **yum**" was even better.

Then Henry's mother said
she wanted some sweet, fresh corn.
"Yum yum **yum**!" said Henry.
Mudge wagged so hard that
he knocked a chair over.

"Does this mean we're going
to a farm?" Henry asked his mother.
"I hope so," said Henry's dad.
He picked up the chair.
"One more yum and Mudge may
knock the whole house down."

"Wow!" said Henry. "We're going
to a farm, Mudge!"
Henry could hardly wait.

Welcome!

Henry and Mudge and Henry's parents
drove to the country.

They passed fields and barns.

They passed tractors and haystacks.

133

And once they had to stop
to let a duck and her children
cross the road.

Mudge wanted to get out of
the car and kiss the ducks.
But Henry wouldn't let him.
"No, Mudge," Henry said.
"No kisses."

Mudge kissed Henry instead.

Soon Henry's mother said,
"There's the sign!"
The sign said,
FRENCH'S FARM
2 MILES.
"Yay!" said Henry.

Henry's father drove up
to the farmhouse.
It was white and clean
and flowery.

FRENCH'S FARM

OPEN

"Look at those big sunflowers!"
said Henry.
"Everything is bigger in
the country," said Henry's mother.

They all got out of the car.

A woman wearing an apron

came from the house.

"Welcome!" she said. "I'm

Mrs. French."

Mrs. French was nice.
She told Henry he could walk
all around the farm.
She said that he could take Mudge.

CORN
~~ lb.

$5
A
BUNCH

While they explored,
Henry's parents would get eggs
and blueberries and corn
and all kinds of other
good farm things.

142

"Let's go, Mudge!" said Henry.
Mudge wagged and off they went.

144

The Chase

Henry and Mudge met a lot
of farm animals.
They met a goat that tried
to eat Henry's shirt.

They met chickens that
pecked Mudge's head.
(He didn't feel the pecks.
Mudge had a head like concrete.)

They met a shy cat and her kittens.

They met a sheep.

And then they met a goose.

"Uh-oh," said Henry.

"HONK!" said the goose.

"HONK! HONK! HONK!"

"Geese are very grumpy,"
Henry told Mudge.

"HONK! HONK! HONK!"

The goose was not happy
to see them.

He honked and honked and honked.
Mudge didn't like it.
He tried to hide between
Henry's legs.
"Yikes!" said Henry,
falling over.

The goose honked Henry and Mudge
all the way back
to the farmhouse.

They ran inside.
Henry's parents were paying
Mrs. French for the
bag of eggs and berries
and corn they were
taking home.

152

Henry's father looked
at Henry and Mudge.
He looked at the goose
honking outside the window.
"Looks like you've been
on a wild goose chase,"
he told Henry.

"Yes, but we weren't
doing the chasing!"
said Henry.

Mudge and the goose
looked at each other
through the window.
"Honk," said the goose.

Mudge looked.
"Honk," said the goose.
Mudge looked.
"Honk," said the goose.

"BARK!"
said Mudge.

157

The goose jumped three feet
in the air and went running
wildly away!

"You're right, Mom,"
Henry said, laughing.
"Everything **is** bigger in
the country.

Especially Mudge's **bark**!"
Mudge wagged proudly.
And Henry gave him
a farm-fresh kiss.

HENRY AND MUDGE
AND THE
FUNNY LUNCH

Contents

Mother's Day

One day in May, Henry and Henry's
big dog, Mudge, were playing kickball
with some friends.

(Kickball was better than catch
because no one had to pick up the
drooly ball.)

165

Suddenly Henry remembered something:
Mother's Day!
Henry and his dad always made a funny
lunch for Henry's mother on Mother's Day.

One year they made a Tomato Snowman.

Another year they baked a
Sweet Potato Shoe.

Mother's Day was only a day away.
What would they make for lunch this year?

"Let's go find Dad, Mudge," Henry
said, heading home.
Mudge shook hands with all of
Henry's friends before leaving.
Mudge had very good manners.

Henry's father hadn't forgotten Mother's Day.

When Henry got home, his dad was making a grocery list.

"What are we fixing for Mother's Day lunch?" Henry asked.

Henry's father smiled.

"Something juicy," he said.

Mudge wagged.

He liked juicy things.

"Something crunchy," said
Henry's father.
Mudge wagged again.
He liked crunchy things, too.

"Something you can really stretch out on!" Henry's father said.
"Something juicy and crunchy that you can stretch out on?" asked Henry.
"What in the world is it?"

"A Pineapple Sofa!"
said Henry's father.

Mudge wagged and wagged and wagged. "Juicy" and "Crunchy" and "Sofa" were some of his favorite words!

Shopping

Henry and Mudge went grocery shopping with Henry's father. The grocery store owner was a cousin of Henry's father, so he always let Mudge in.

Mudge *loved* grocery shopping.

He got crackers as soon as he came through the door. While Henry and Henry's father bought things for a Pineapple Sofa, Mudge walked around and sniffed.

He sniffed and sniffed and sniffed.

He sniffed the Fruity Puffs.

He sniffed the Cocoa Chews.

He even sniffed the Fishy Flakes.

No one minded because everyone in the
store loved Mudge.

184

Babies gave him their suckers and grandmas rubbed his head.
They were all glad to see him.

Soon the shopping was done.

Henry and Mudge and Henry's father
headed home.

Henry and his dad laughed about the
Pineapple Sofa they were going to make.

Henry's dad said that maybe it should be a sleep sofa.

He said that maybe it should pull out into a Watermelon Bed.

Henry giggled and giggled.

He loved making funny food.

189

Yum!

On Mother's Day Henry and
Henry's father got to work.
They cut pineapple cushions.
They fixed marshmallow pillows.

They made an apple father,

a peach mother,

a plum boy,

and a kiwi dog.

Then they set everything on top of a giant chocolate bar and served it to Henry's mother.

"Happy Mother's Day!" said Henry.

"Yum!" said Henry's mother, clapping
her hands.

She shared the Pineapple Sofa with everyone,
then gave each of them a big kiss.

Later, as they rested on their *real* sofa, Henry's father said to Henry, "What if next year we do a French Fry Cat?"

Mudge wagged and wagged
and wagged.